The Stolen Kitten

The Stolen Kitten

by Holly Webb
Illustrated by Katherine Kirkland

tiger tales

tiger tales

5 River Road, Suite 128, Wilton, CT 06897
Published in the United States 2018
Originally published in Great Britain 2011
as *Smudge the Stolen Kitten* by the Little Tiger Group
Text copyright © 2011 Holly Webb
Cover illustration copyright © 2011 Sophy Williams
Interior illustrations copyright © 2011 Katherine Kirkland
ISBN-13: 978-1-68010-429-5
ISBN-10: 1-68010-429-2
Printed in China
STP/1800/0329/1219
All rights reserved
10 9 8 7 6 5 4 3 2

For more insight and activities, visit us at www.tigertalesbooks.com

Contents

For Robin

Chapter One
Exciting News

There was the sound of a whistle blowing. "Ben Williams and Rob Ford! Get down from there right now!"

Olivia looked up and groaned. Mrs. Macintosh sounded as if she'd yelled right in Olivia's ear, even though she was on the other side of the playground.

"What have Ben and Rob done now?" her friend Hailey asked.

"Something awful, as usual," Olivia muttered as they ran across the playground to see what was going on. Her older brother, Ben, was always in trouble at school—which wasn't fair, because all the teachers either thought that meant Olivia was naughty, too, or that she should have stopped him. As if he'd listen to her! And his friend Rob was even worse.

"You're very lucky you haven't broken your necks!" the girls heard Mrs. Macintosh saying angrily. "What a careless thing to do!"

"It isn't in the playground rules that we can't tightrope walk along the top of the fence, Mrs. Macintosh," Ben said innocently, pointing to the poster on the side of the wall.

"That's because before you, Ben, no one had even thought of it!" the teacher snapped. "We need to add an extra rule at the bottom of that list saying that whatever crazy thing you two think of next isn't allowed! You can miss the rest of recess. Go inside and tell Mrs. Beale that you're going to help set up the chairs for the assembly this afternoon!"

Ben winked at Olivia as he and Rob went past on their way back inside. He didn't look like he minded being scolded at all.

Olivia sighed, and Hailey gave her a sympathetic smile. "It's probably better than having a brother who's totally perfect—then everyone would ask you why you couldn't be more like him."

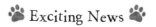

"I suppose," Olivia sighed, kicking at a pile of leaves. "But I can't wait until he goes to high school next year."

"Mrs. Beale told me about what happened at lunchtime, by the way." Mom eyed Ben sternly. She worked as a part-time teaching assistant at Olivia and Ben's school.

Ben waved a forkful of spaghetti at her, looking hurt. "It's so unfair! No one had ever said we couldn't walk along the fence."

"Sometimes I think we should just send you and Rob to join the circus." Dad was trying to look angry, but Olivia could see that he was smiling.

"Excellent! No more school!" Ben grinned.

"Stop acting smart, Ben." Mom frowned. "I'm tempted not to tell you the special news I got."

Olivia looked up from her pasta. "What is it? Don't be mean, Mom!"

Her mom stared up at the ceiling, smiling, while Olivia and Ben begged her to tell.

"All right, all right! You remember a while ago there was a flyer through the door about the cat rescue center in town?"

Olivia nodded eagerly. "With photos of all the cats they'd found new homes for! They were beautiful. I wish we could have one. It said they always needed good homes for unwanted cats."

Mom smiled. "I know, Olivia—you went on about it for days. Well, Dad and I have been talking, and we decided that maybe you're both old enough to have a pet."

"Really?" Olivia gasped. "We're going to get a cat?"

"I'd rather have a dog, Mom," Ben put in. "Dogs are more fun."

Mom shook her head. "No. Dad's at work all day, and you're both at school, and so am I three days a week. A dog would get really lonely."

Ben sighed and nodded, so Mom went on quickly. "I gave the center a call this morning. They've got some kittens at the moment who are ready for new homes now."

Olivia jumped up, almost knocking

her pasta into her lap. "Let's go!"

"Livvy, sit down!" Mom laughed. "The center isn't even open right now. And anyway, before we can go and choose a kitten, we have to have a home visit. To make sure that we're going to be suitable owners."

Olivia sat down, staring back at Mom worriedly. "Suitable? What does that mean? Do we have to know a lot about cats? I only know a bit. But I've got lots of books about cats, and we could look things up on the computer...."

"Slow down!" Dad patted her shoulder. "It's okay. They're just going to want to check that our street isn't too busy. And that we're okay with putting a cat flap in the kitchen door, that kind of thing."

"And that we don't have children who won't know how to behave around a cat," Mom said, eyeing Ben grimly. "A lady from the center is coming to see us tonight, and we'll all have to show her that we're well behaved,

Benjamin Williams."

Ben scowled, and Olivia looked at him warily. Ben wasn't sensible at all. In fact, he was the least sensible person Olivia had ever met.

How were they ever going to convince the lady from the rescue center that they were the right owners for a kitten?

"I'll give you this week's allowance," Olivia said desperately.

Ben raised one eyebrow.

"And my Saturday treats, too! But you have to promise to be on your absolute best behavior. Actually, don't even talk! Or—or move!"

Ben zipped his lips with his fingers and smirked at her, but Olivia wasn't sure she could trust him.

"Oh, there's the doorbell! Should we answer it, or let Mom?" Olivia twisted her fingers together nervously. She really wanted to make a good impression.

"Mmmpfl." Ben made a strange grunting noise, and Olivia stared at him.

He shrugged. "Well, you said not to talk!"

"That doesn't mean make silly noises! If she asks you a question, you have to say something."

"Something."

"Fine, I'm keeping my allowance." Olivia marched down the stairs feeling furious. If Ben managed to mess this up, she was never going to forgive him. Ben followed her, snickering.

Mom was just opening the door to a friendly-looking lady in a Rescue Center fleece.

"Hi. I'm Debbie, from the Cat Rescue Center."

"Thanks for coming. I'm Elaine, and this is my husband, John, and this is Olivia and Ben." Mom led Debbie into the living room, and Olivia and Ben followed behind. Dad went to put the kettle on for tea.

"It seems like a fairly quiet area." Debbie made a note on the sheet she was holding. "Not too many cars."

"A lot of people around here have cats," Olivia put in hopefully.

Mom laughed. "And Olivia is friends with all of them!"

Olivia perched nervously on the edge of the couch. Ben was sitting on its arm, and for once he didn't look like he was planning anything silly. Olivia crossed her fingers. "Are there really kittens at the rescue center right now?" she asked Debbie shyly.

Debbie nodded. "Two litters, actually. One's mostly orange and white, and the others are a smokey gray. They're all really sweet."

Olivia's eyes shone as she imagined sitting on the couch, just like she was now, but with a tiny gray kitten purring on her lap.

Debbie went through a long list of questions, checking how much time the kitten would be left alone, and that Olivia's mom knew they'd have to pay for vet bills. Olivia could see the list if she leaned over, and it mostly had checks in the boxes. Hopefully Debbie would say yes!

Just as Debbie was handing Mom some flyers about pet insurance and flea treatments, Dad came in with a tray of tea. He passed the cups around, then he sat down on the couch next to Olivia. There was a sudden, very loud, very rude noise, and Dad jumped up, his face scarlet.

Ben practically fell off the couch arm because he was laughing so much, and Olivia pulled out a whoopee cushion from behind Dad.

"Ben!" Mom sounded horrified.

"I forgot it was there, sorry," Ben said, but he didn't look very sorry.

Olivia looked at Debbie, her eyes starting to burn with tears. Did having a naughty big brother mean no kitten?

But Debbie was giggling. "Wow, I haven't seen one of those in years. My brother used to do that all the time." Then she looked serious. "A kitten really is a big responsibility, though. And everyone in the family has to be prepared to help care for it properly." She was staring at Ben, who looked embarrassed.

"I will take good care of it. I promise," he muttered.

Debbie nodded. "Okay then." She signed her name in swirly letters across the bottom of the form. "You can come and choose your kitten tomorrow!"

Chapter Two
A New Home

Olivia doodled in her notebook, trying to think of the best name for a beautiful little gray kitten, or maybe a sweet orange one. She liked Esmeralda as an option. But then Dad had said at breakfast that it had to be a name that they didn't mind yelling across the yard to get the kitten to come in to eat. Olivia giggled. She couldn't really see Ben shouting, "Es-mer-al-da!"

Fluffy? Patches? Whiskers? None of them sounded quite right. Olivia scowled down at the picture she was drawing. A kitten with big, sad eyes, just waiting for her to come and bring him home. She wished they'd been able to go to the Rescue Center yesterday, right after Debbie had approved them, but Mom said they needed to get everything ready first, and Olivia supposed she was right. They didn't even have a food bowl!

Hailey elbowed her in the ribs. "Mr. Jones is looking at you, Olivia!"

Olivia straightened up and tried to look as though she was listening. She usually loved history, but today she couldn't think of anything except

24

kittens. They were going to the pet store after school to get everything, and then on to the Rescue Center!

The kitten finished his bowl of food and licked his paw, swiping it across his nose and ears. Then he trotted over to the wire front of the pen and stood up on his hind paws, his front claws scraping on the wire. He scratched at it for a moment, hoping that someone might come and open it for him. Sometimes the Rescue Center staff came to play with the kittens when they weren't too busy. But maybe they wouldn't, now that it was only him.

He unhooked his claws and padded

sadly back to the cushion on the shelf in the corner. It was too big for just him—until yesterday, three small gray kittens had shared it, and now when he curled up he was lost in the middle. He missed his sisters. Even though the Center was warm, he still felt chilly all on his own.

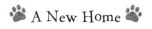

"The kittens are this way." Debbie smiled at Olivia and Ben, and their mom and dad. "You haven't changed your minds, have you? You'd still like one?" she teased.

"Yes!" Olivia nodded so hard her pigtails shook up and down. "And we've got a cat basket and a litter box and a grooming brush and some toys and two bowls!"

Debbie laughed. "You just need the kitten then! Come on." She led the way down the hall, which was lined with wire-fronted enclosures. They were full of cats, all watching as Olivia walked past. She blinked, feeling suddenly sad. It wasn't that the little pens weren't nice—the cats each had a basket and toys, and most of the pens were built with a shelf so the cats could be high up, where they felt safe. But they weren't a real home. She wondered how often they got cuddled or petted.

"We do take them all out every day. At least once," Debbie said quietly.

Olivia blinked. How had Debbie known what she was thinking?

"I know it doesn't look very cozy, but it's better than being out in the cold." Debbie sighed. "I'd like to take every single one home, but I already have five cats.... I can't really have any more...." She shook herself, and smiled firmly. "Look. The two litters of kittens are in the large pens down this side."

"Oh...." Olivia crouched down in

front of the wire pen.

Four orange kittens were bouncing here and there, chasing each other around a scratching post and up onto a shelf where a white cat, who Olivia guessed was their mother, was trying to sleep. They scrambled over her—she looked as though she was used to it by now, and her ears didn't even twitch— and then jumped down and did it all over again.

"My goodness," Mom muttered. "They're very energetic, aren't they?"

Olivia looked at her anxiously. She hoped Mom wasn't changing her mind. "We're only going to have one," she pointed out, her voice a little squeaky with worry. "They only look bouncy because there are so many of them."

Debbie nodded. "Kittens are very energetic, but Olivia's right. Just one won't be quite so crazy. Look, we have one gray kitten left in the pen further down. He's a bit calmer."

Olivia had been so excited seeing the beautiful orange kittens that she'd almost forgotten there was one more.

"There were three in this litter, but two of them were adopted yesterday. I think this one's feeling a little lonely." Debbie beckoned them along the hallway to the enclosure, where a small kitten was stretched out on his sleeping shelf, licking a paw and looking sad. He glanced up as Olivia and her family came closer, and Olivia laughed delightedly. His round green eyes gave him a permanent surprised look, and he had beautiful, thick gray fur the color of a puff of smoke.

The kitten jumped down from his sleeping shelf and padded over to the wire front of the pen.

"He's so beautiful, Mom," Olivia whispered. "Look at him! He's so cute, with his little tail!"

"He is very sweet," Mom agreed.

The kitten meowed hopefully. He liked Debbie, and he knew she usually came to feed him and pet him. And he liked the look of the other people, too. Maybe they'd pick him up. They might even take him with them. Someone had taken his sisters, so why not him?

"Where did he come from?" Dad asked. "You don't have his mom as well, like the other kittens?"

Debbie shook her head and sighed. "No…." She glanced at Ben and Olivia, as though she didn't want to upset them. "These kittens were abandoned. A lady out for a walk by the canal found them. Someone had just left them in a cardboard box."

Olivia stared at the kitten, who was pawing hopefully at the wire. How could someone have abandoned him?

"They were lucky to be found so quickly," Debbie added. "They were only two weeks old; they would have died if they'd been left much longer without food." She patted Olivia's arm, seeing how upset she was. "But the good thing about it is that the kittens were bottle-fed, which means they're super-friendly. This one is a little love. He wants to be cuddled all the time."

"Can we have him?" Olivia turned around. "Ben, don't you think he's beautiful?"

"I guess so. The orange ones were really fun, but he looks friendly, too," Ben said.

"Let's get him out so you can pet him," Debbie suggested.

"Oh, yes, please...." Olivia gazed through the wire at the kitten. He was scratching at it now, looking as though he liked the idea, too. Debbie opened the front of the pen and laughed as he scampered out before she could catch him.

The kitten skidded to a stop in front of Olivia's feet and glanced up, suddenly shy. He looked at Olivia sideways, obviously wondering who she was and if she was friendly.

Olivia stretched out her fingers to him and he sniffed them, and then rubbed the side of his face up and down her hand. "Aww! Do you think I could pick him up?" she asked Debbie.

"Give it a try. Don't worry if he wriggles away because he'll probably be a little excited."

But the kitten snuggled happily against Olivia's school sweater and purred. This was just what he wanted. So much better than being all alone in the pen, and the girl smelled nice.

Olivia rubbed him gently behind the ears. His fur was soft and velvety, and he nuzzled a tiny, cold pink nose into her neck, making her giggle. "Oh, listen to him purring! He sounds like a little lawn mower!"

The kitten closed his eyes happily and kneaded his paws into Olivia's shoulder.

Debbie smiled. "He's definitely taken to you."

Olivia's eyes glowed as she looked up at her parents, kitten paws tangled in her sweater. "Can we have him? Please?"

"What about the orange ones?" Ben grumbled, but then he petted the top of the kitten's head. "I guess he is cute," he admitted.

Dad nodded, smiling. "So, what are we going to call him?"

In the end, the name was obvious. Smokey just fit. Olivia's mom suggested Alfie, and Ben wanted to name him after his favorite soccer player, but Smokey just looked like Smokey.

He fit into the house, too. Debbie had said that he was already house-trained. She'd also explained that Smokey had had all his vaccinations, so it was safe to let him go outside, but it would be better not to let him out on his own for the first couple of weeks until he got used to his new home. Dad was glad about that, as it gave him a little longer to fit the cat flap.

On his first night, Olivia had left Smokey curled up in his new basket.

She'd lined up all his toys next to him and given him one of her old toy cats in case he was lonely. Then she'd refilled his water bowl and given him a chicken-flavored cat treat as a bedtime snack.

"Olivia, it's way past your bedtime!" Mom put an arm around her shoulders. "He'll be fine. He's used to the Rescue Center. I'm sure our kitchen is much nicer than that pen he was in."

Olivia nodded. "Yes, but he doesn't know our house yet, and he doesn't understand what's happening. What if he thinks we're never coming back?"

"Come on. You're not sleeping in the kitchen with him, Livvy."

Olivia sighed and looked back sadly as Mom shooed her out. The light from the hallway gleamed in the kitten's huge eyes. He looked sad, too.

Upstairs, Olivia got ready for bed. But she couldn't stop thinking about Smokey, alone in the dark kitchen. Maybe she should just go and check on him....

Ben was lying on his bed reading, and he glanced up as Olivia went past. "Mom will hear if you sneak downstairs, Olivia. She always catches me."

Olivia leaned around his bedroom door. "How did you know what I was doing?" she hissed. "I might just have been going to the bathroom!"

Ben shrugged. "I could tell by the way you were looking at the stairs." He frowned. "Hey, is that Smokey making that noise?"

From downstairs came a faint but pitiful wailing, along with a scratching sound. The noise of kitten claws scratching at a kitchen door.

Olivia hung over the banister, listening to the sad little howls.

Eventually, Mom came out of the living room, frowning. "I hope he's all right," she said over her shoulder to Dad. "Oh, Olivia. Is he keeping you awake?"

"Can't we let him come upstairs?" Olivia pleaded. "He sounds so lonely."

Mom sighed and glanced at Dad.

Dad shrugged. "Well, he is house-trained."

"Thank you!" Olivia smiled with delight and ran down the stairs to open the kitchen door.

Smokey shot out, and she gathered him into her arms, cuddling him against her pajamas. "Don't worry, Smokey," she whispered. "I'll take care of you." She carried him upstairs and put him down gently on her bed.

Smokey looked around interestedly, and padded up and down Olivia's comforter, inspecting it carefully. Olivia tried not to laugh. He looked so serious. Then he marched over to her pillow, curled himself up in the hollow between the pillow and the comforter, and went to sleep.

Chapter Three
The Exploring Begins

Smokey had only been there a few days, but Olivia's house was definitely his home now. He had explored every possible hole and hiding place, and gotten stuck in several of them. But Olivia or Ben or their parents were always there to rescue him. Except for today. Dad was at work, Olivia and Ben had gone to school that morning, and as it was Thursday, their mom had to go into school to work, too. Smokey was on his own for the first time, and he didn't like it. He wandered around the house, his tail twitching. He'd already been into every room that was open, and he knew that no one was there, but he kept hoping that maybe if he looked again he would find somebody.

He padded back into the kitchen and sniffed hopefully at the door. Olivia and Ben had taken him out into the yard when they got home from school yesterday. It had been his first taste of the outside world, and his ears flickered back and forth as he remembered watching the birds, and chasing after the little jingly ball that Olivia had rolled along the patio.

There it was, in the corner by the kitchen cupboards. Smokey trotted over and patted the ball with one paw. It rolled along, the little bell jingling, and he pounced on it. The ball slid along the polished tiles, and so did Smokey, rolling over onto his back, wriggling and clawing at it. But then the ball slid away from his paws and stopped against the kitchen table leg, and it wasn't as much fun anymore.

Grumpily, Smokey lay there on his back, licking his paws. He'd already had a long nap in the recycling box next to the kitchen counter. (Ben had emptied it that morning, and it was just the right size for Smokey to feel cozy in—much better than his basket.) Now he wanted someone to play with.

Maybe by the time he got upstairs, Olivia would be back in her bedroom! He trotted through to the hallway and started to struggle up the stairs. He was big enough to climb them, but it was an effort, and he had to scramble and scratch and pull himself up each step. He sat down for a little while at the top of the stairs, his sides heaving, and then he crept along the landing and nosed his way around the door to Olivia's bedroom.

She wasn't there. The room was empty.

Smokey crept under Olivia's bed. He picked his way between two tottering piles of books and pounced on Olivia's hair dryer. Then, yawning, he snuggled himself inside her gym bag. He liked small spaces, and climbing the stairs had worn him out. When he woke up, surely they would all be back....

"I can't believe it's only lunchtime," Olivia muttered, checking her watch for the hundredth time.

"Are you missing Smokey?" Hailey grinned at her.

Olivia nodded. "It's the first time we've left him alone all day. I really hope he's okay. He almost climbed out of the living room window yesterday. I caught him just as he was sticking his head out."

"He still isn't allowed outside? Isn't he old enough?"

"He's 10 weeks old, so he could go outside, but Debbie said it's best if we wait until we've had him a little longer before letting him out on his own. It already feels like he's been with us forever, though. He isn't shy or nervous at all." Then she shook her head. "Except for yesterday, when we took Smokey into the yard with us, and Ben got him with his water squirter. He said it was an accident, but I don't know...."

Hailey sighed. "I'm so jealous. I love Tigger, but he's really old and just sleeps all day. Can I come and see Smokey soon?" she asked hopefully.

Olivia nodded. She was desperate to show off how handsome Smokey was. "Do you want to come tomorrow? Mom's doing playground duty, so we could go and ask her."

They ran over to Olivia's mom, who was turning the end of a jump rope for a bunch of girls. "Mom, can Hailey come over tomorrow? She really wants to see Smokey."

Mom frowned. "Oh, not on Friday, Hailey, I'm sorry. Ben has invited Rob around already. I'll ask your mom about coming over this weekend," she suggested, and Hailey nodded, looking pleased, but Olivia was frowning.

"Rob's coming over? Mom, does

he have to? Ben always goofs around when he's with Rob. They'll be awful! They might upset Smokey!"

"I'm sure they won't, Olivia. Oh, dear! Let me help you, Hannah!" One of the younger girls had tripped over the rope, and Mom went to pick her up.

Olivia sighed and glanced at Hailey. "I bet they will. You know what Ben's like. And with Rob there, he's three times as bad. I'll just have to keep Smokey with me the entire time."

"Smokey! Where are you, kitty?" As soon as Olivia got home from school, she dropped her bag, pulled off her coat, and dashed upstairs to search for him. Maybe he was taking a nap on her bed. As she pushed her bedroom door wide open, there was a little meow, and Smokey wriggled out from under her bed. A pile of books toppled over as he shot out and scrambled into her lap. Olivia giggled. "Mom's right—I really do need to clean up, especially if you're going to go exploring under there. Those books almost squashed your tail!" She settled down to do her homework with Smokey purring on her knee. When she finished, she carried him downstairs and wandered into the kitchen to talk to Mom. Ben was out in the yard building a fort in the apple tree.

"Mom, does Rob have to come over tomorrow?"

Mom looked up from the sauce she was stirring. "Well, yes. It's all arranged. What's the matter, Livvy?"

Olivia shrugged. "I don't want him to...," she whispered. "He does crazy stuff, and he makes Ben do crazy stuff, too. They always get into trouble."

Mom sighed. "I know they misbehave sometimes. But Rob is Ben's best friend. Can't you just stay out of their way tomorrow?"

"But what if they upset Smokey? Can I take him up to my room tomorrow to keep him out of their way, too?"

Mom looked at her seriously for a moment, then shook her head. "Olivia, Ben wants to show Smokey to Rob. I know you really love Smokey, and he's taken to you so well, but he's not just yours, sweetheart. He's Ben's kitten, too."

Olivia nodded miserably. She knew Mom was right, but it didn't help. It felt like Smokey was her kitten, and she didn't want the boys anywhere near him.

"Hello, Smokey!" Olivia's dad walked in and tickled the kitten under the chin.

Then Ben flung open the kitchen door and stomped muddy footprints across the floor. "Is it dinnertime yet?"

"Shoes off!" Mom grabbed him. "And then it is, yes."

Olivia rolled her eyes at Mom. "You see?" she muttered. She put Smokey down on the floor and went to help pass the bowls of pasta around.

"What?" Ben asked, as he hopped around, taking off his sneakers.

Olivia folded her arms. "I just don't think it's a good idea for you to have Rob over tomorrow. Not when we've only had Smokey for three days. Rob will probably get Smokey to … to climb trees or something. You always do crazy things with him! Like that time you dug a tunnel and pulled up all Dad's daffodil bulbs!"

Ben shook his head. "That's so not fair! For starters, we didn't know they were there! And anyway, Rob loves cats. He's been asking his mom and dad for one for months. He can't wait to meet Smokey."

"Oh…," Olivia muttered.

"Actually, where is Smokey?" Mom asked.

Olivia looked down, expecting to see him by her feet, hoping to be fed. But he wasn't there.

"I don't know." Olivia went to look in the hallway, but then there was a worried little meow from somewhere on the other side of the kitchen.

Mom frowned. "Where on earth is he?"

The meowing got louder.

"I think he's behind the oven!" Ben said suddenly.

"But it's still hot from cooking dinner!" Mom cried.

Olivia dashed over to the oven. "Smokey, come out of there!"

But Smokey only meowed louder.

"He's stuck," Olivia muttered, crouching down and trying to reach behind the oven. "Ow, and it's hot. I can't get to him. I think he got trapped and now he can't turn around!"

Dad shook his head. "What is it with that kitten? The smaller the space, the more he likes it. I'll have to pull the oven out a bit."

55

He dragged the oven out from the wall, and Smokey darted out and ran to Olivia. He was trembling and covered in dust balls—he looked even furrier than usual.

Mom shook her head. "I don't think Smokey needs the boys to get him into trouble, Olivia. He can manage it perfectly well on his own!"

Chapter Four
Rob's Idea

After school on Friday, Olivia ran into the house ahead of Rob and Ben, looking for Smokey.

The little gray kitten slipped around the living room door, meowing excitedly, and purred as she picked him up. Olivia petted him lovingly, and then took a step back as Rob came over to her. She was used to Rob racing around the playground with Ben, chasing people and getting into trouble. She wasn't sure he knew how to be careful with a kitten.

"Hey! He's really cute!"

Olivia nodded slowly.

"Can I pet him? Will he mind?" Even Rob's voice was gentler than usual.

"Um, okay…." Olivia looked on anxiously, but Rob tickled Smokey behind the ears—his favorite place, and Smokey purred and wriggled so much that Olivia had to hand him over, letting him fasten his claws in Rob's school sweater.

"He likes you!" Ben commented. "Come on, bring him up to my room." He grabbed Smokey's favorite jingly ball and a squeaky mouse.

"But...." Olivia watched as the boys thundered up the stairs, taking Smokey with them. She started to run after them, but Mom called her back.

"Leave them alone, Olivia."

"But they took Smokey up there. What are they going to do with him?"

Mom laughed. "Just play with him, like you do! Rob seems to really like him. Come on, Livvy. Come and make some chocolate-chip cookies with me. We can have them after dinner."

Olivia sighed. She supposed Mom was right. Maybe she was just feeling jealous because Smokey seemed to like Rob.

They were in the middle of cutting out the cookies when Ben and Rob and Smokey came down to watch TV.

Olivia looked at Smokey carefully, but he seemed to be all right. The boys hadn't trimmed his whiskers, or painted him blue, or done any of the other silly things she'd been imagining.

A little later, Ben came into the kitchen. "Are the cookies ready yet? They smell fantastic."

"The first batch is almost done, but they're for after dinner, Ben! We're having fish sticks. And I can see you stealing the chocolate!" Mom waved a spoon at him as Ben popped a handful of chocolate chips into his mouth, grinning.

"Where's Smokey?" Olivia asked anxiously.

"Sitting on the couch with Rob— calm down, Olivia! He's fine. Rob thinks he's great."

Olivia stared out of the kitchen door, hoping Smokey might come in to see her. But he stayed with Rob.

Smokey yawned and stretched out his paws. Rob was petting him very nicely, but he wanted to go and see what Olivia was doing. He hadn't seen her all day, and he wanted her to play with him. And he was hungry. There were food smells coming from the kitchen. *Good fishy smells*, he thought. He stood up sleepily, getting ready to jump off Rob's lap.

Rob looked down. "Where are you going, Smokey?" He tickled him under the chin, and Smokey purred. Maybe he wouldn't go just yet.

"Ben's so lucky," Rob whispered gently. "I wish I had a kitten like you." He sighed and picked up his school bag from the floor, rooting around in it.

Smokey peered over and stuck his nose in. It smelled good.

Rob laughed. "I'm just looking for my gum, but I don't think you'll want that. Oh, I bet I know what you can smell. My leftover ham sandwich." He laughed again as Smokey stuck his entire head in the bag. "Where are you going?"

Smokey could smell the delicious ham at the bottom of the bag, and he wriggled all the way in.

"Hey, Ben's going to think I'm taking

you home." Rob grinned. But then his smile faded a little. Smokey popped his head out of the bag, licking around his jaws hopefully. "There isn't any more, Smokey, sorry."

The little kitten yawned and ducked back into the school bag, curling up at the bottom and closing his eyes.

Rob shook his head. "I can't believe you're asleep in my bag." He stared at Smokey thoughtfully and sighed. "I really could take you home...."

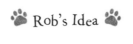

 Rob's Idea

"Mrs. Williams...."

"Oh, hello, Rob. Do you want to help with the cookies?"

Rob was standing by the kitchen door, looking uncomfortable. "Um. No. I have to go home. Um, I feel sick."

"Oh, dear!" Olivia's mom put down the tray of cookies and hurried over to him.

Ben and Olivia stared at Rob in surprise. "You don't look sick," Ben said.

"Has it just suddenly come over you?" Olivia's mom asked. "Are you hot?"

Rob backed away from her and nodded. "Yes. And I feel really sick. Please can I call my mom?"

"Of course." She handed him the phone. "You poor thing."

Rob took the phone out into the hallway, and they could hear him explaining urgently to his mom.

"He does sound very upset, poor Rob," Olivia's mom said anxiously.

"He was fine 10 minutes ago," Ben muttered.

Olivia frowned. "I bet he broke something. And he doesn't want to get into trouble. Did he mess anything up in your room?"

"Don't be silly, Olivia. The boys have just been watching TV. How could he have broken anything?" Mom glared at her angrily. "You shouldn't be mean."

"She's coming." Rob stood at the

kitchen door, holding out the phone to Olivia's mom.

Rob's mom arrived a few minutes later, and Olivia's mom chatted with her, while Rob lurked impatiently by the door. "I'm really sorry. I don't think it's anything he's eaten—we hadn't even had dinner."

Rob's mom shook her head. "It's probably just something going around—I only hope he hasn't given it to Ben and Olivia. At least he's got the weekend to recover. Anyway, I'd better get him home. Thank you for having him!"

Rob darted into the living room and came out carrying his school bag. He was holding it against his tummy, hunching over, and his mom looked at him worriedly. "Oh, dear, you do look like you might be sick. Come on, let's get you home." She led him down the front path to the car.

Mom closed the door and hurried into the kitchen. "I forgot about the fish sticks with all of that going on; I'm afraid they might be a bit crispy…."

"Can Smokey have one of Rob's?" Olivia asked. "I bet he'd love a fish stick." Then she jumped up suddenly. "Where is Smokey?" she asked, her voice a little panicky. "I haven't seen him in a while. Rob was cuddling him in the living room."

"Maybe Rob shut the living room door?" Mom suggested, as she served dinner. "He might be stuck in there."

But the living room door was open,

and there was no Smokey on the couch, or hiding behind it to leap out at Olivia as she searched around. She darted upstairs to look in her room.

"Smokey! Smokey! Mom, he's not in there, and I've checked upstairs, and I can't find him anywhere!" Olivia ran back into the kitchen.

Ben was sitting at the table eating a huge pile of fish sticks—his and Rob's. "He's probably under your bed or something. I'll come and help you look." But Smokey wasn't in either of their rooms, and he hadn't climbed into the bathtub and got stuck. He wasn't in the pantry, either.

"Could he have gotten out somehow?" Ben asked when they came back downstairs.

Mom frowned. "I'm sure all the windows were shut. After he almost got out yesterday, I was worried he might try that again."

Olivia nodded. "I checked all the windows this morning before we went to school."

Mom sighed. "Smokey must be hiding

somewhere, like he always does. He'll pop out at us in a minute, I'm sure."

Olivia turned to Ben, her hands on her hips. "Did you and Rob let him outside?"

Ben stared at her, wide-eyed. "He was just watching TV with us, Olivia. We didn't even go out, so how is it suddenly our fault?"

"I bet that's why Rob wanted to go home." Olivia sat down on a chair as her knees suddenly felt shaky. "He was scared he was going to get into trouble. You let him out. I can't believe you'd do that!" she yelled.

"Olivia!" Mom warned. "You're jumping to conclusions."

"We didn't let him out!" Ben stood up angrily. "How many times do I have to say it?" He stomped out of the kitchen, muttering. "I'm going to look for him upstairs. He must be here somewhere."

Olivia slumped on her chair, feeling tears welling up in her eyes. No matter how much Ben denied it, she was sure the boys had let Smokey get out— either by accident, or as part of some ridiculous game. Smokey was so little! He'd only been outside once, and he'd had Ben and her there to make sure he didn't escape from the yard, or get himself stuck somewhere. Just thinking of all the places where he might hurt himself made her feel sick.

Chapter Five
Searching for Smokey

Smokey woke up and was surprised to find that everything was dark, and the bag was bumping around. The little kitten swayed from side to side, meowing with fright. Where was Olivia? Why was he stuck in here? He needed Olivia to let him out!

"Hey, shhh. I'm going to get you out of there."

The bag opened, and Smokey could see Rob peering inside. He gave a soft little meow. This wasn't right. He had thought that Olivia would come and find him. He cowered back against the bottom of the bag and hissed as Rob tried to open it up a little more. The boy had been kind before, petting and cuddling him, and feeding him sandwiches, but now Smokey was confused, and he wanted Olivia.

"Hey, Smokey. Don't you want to get out? Come and see my bedroom," Rob said, gently reaching in to pick up the kitten.

Smokey spat angrily as a warning, and when Rob didn't take his hand out of the bag, he batted at it with his claw, hard.

"Ow!" Rob sat back, sucking at the bleeding scratch. Then he sighed. "Okay. I suppose I'd scratch if I got trapped in a bag and bounced around all over the place. Maybe I'd better get you something else to eat." He smiled at Smokey. "You liked that ham sandwich, didn't you?"

Smokey saw him stand up.

"I'll go and see what's in the fridge, but I might be a while. Mom still thinks I'm sick, so I'll have to wait until she's not looking. I'll be back soon. Here, you can play with this ball. It's got spikes! That'd be fun, wouldn't it? See you in a minute, Smokey."

The bedroom door clicked and Smokey waited, his heart thumping. Was the boy gone? Was it safe to come out?

Slowly, cautiously, he wriggled out of the bag.

"I can't find him anywhere." Ben was standing in the doorway, and his voice had changed. He wasn't angry anymore—he sounded frightened.

"I told you!" Olivia swiped a hand across her eyes. "You must have opened a window, or let him out of the kitchen door, or something!"

"We didn't! You and Mom were in the kitchen the entire time. How could we let him out of here?"

"Ben's right, Olivia. You're not being fair."

"Even if Ben didn't let him out, his silly friend did!" Olivia sobbed. "And now Smokey is lost!"

"I didn't let him out, I promise I didn't, and Rob didn't, either. He would have said if something had happened." Ben's voice was shaking now.

"Both of you calm down. Olivia, try

to stop crying, sweetheart. It's only making you feel worse. Come on. We'll all do another search around the house. Look at yesterday, when Smokey got himself stuck behind the oven! He's around somewhere, I'm sure of it."

Olivia shook her head. "Then why can't we hear him? If he was here and stuck, he'd be meowing, Mom. Wouldn't he?"

Mom got up. "Maybe you're right. If Smokey was shut in somewhere, we'd hear him. We'd better go and check outside. Maybe there's a window open that we've missed."

"I told you!" Olivia wailed. "Rob let him out, he must have."

Even Ben was looking less certain now. "Rob wouldn't just let him out—

I told him Smokey wasn't allowed outside on his own yet...."

They hurried out into the yard, calling and calling, but apart from next door's cat, Pixie, who looked very curiously at them, the yard was empty. It was starting to get dark, and cold. Olivia shivered, thinking of Smokey outside in the chilly wind.

"What about the shed?" Mom suggested, trying to think of places a kitten might find interesting. "Could he have squeezed himself in there somehow?"

The shed door was tightly shut, but they checked anyway. And under the patio furniture, and behind the pile of flowerpots, and even up the cherry tree.

Smokey was nowhere to be found.

"You two stay here, and I'll go and ask Sally next door if she's seen him," Mom said. "Why don't you go and take another look inside?"

"I'm sorry I said you let him out," Olivia muttered as they peered behind the couch. "I know you wouldn't really."

"Do you think he'll be all right?"

Ben asked miserably. "I just don't see where he could be!"

Olivia stood up again and went to check behind the curtains, but then she stopped. "Rob forgot his lunch box," she said slowly, pointing at a blue lunch box down by the side of the couch. "And a bunch of his books. His notebooks and everything...."

Ben frowned. "Why would he take all that stuff out of his bag?"

"His bag.... He was carrying it in a funny way." Olivia stared at Ben, her eyes wide. "Ben, he didn't let Smokey out, he stole him! Rob put Smokey in his school bag and took him home!"

"Don't be silly," Ben said, but he was chewing his thumbnail worriedly. "He wouldn't.... What's he going to do, hide Smokey in his room? I know he really wanted a pet, but he wouldn't steal our cat...."

"I bet you he did," Olivia told him grimly. She heard the sound of the key in the lock, and rushed out into the hallway. "Mom! We think we know where Smokey is!"

Chapter Six
Smokey's Escape

Smokey gazed around the room. He had no idea where he was, but he knew this wasn't home, and he wanted to get away. His ears were laid back, listening for footsteps. But no one was coming. He had to get out and find Olivia. He shook his head, feeling dazed from bumping around in the bag. His nose was still full of the smell of ham sandwich, and the musty scent of the inside of the bag, but there was something else....

The window was open! Smokey's eyes widened a little.

Rob's bed was pushed up against the wall. If he could jump onto that, it was only a small climb to the windowsill. But the bed was very high up. Much higher than the steps on the stairs he'd struggled with. Smokey glanced anxiously at the door. He was sure the boy would be back soon. He had to be quick. With a huge effort, he ran at the bed, hooking his claws into the comforter and scrambling upward furiously. From the top of the bed it didn't look like such a small climb to the windowsill after all, but the

window had long curtains. Smokey
raced up them, his heart hammering,
leaving a pattern of little hooked loops
all the way up. And then he scrambled
up onto the windowsill.

He peered out the open window, his nose twitching, trying to see where to go next. But below him was only a straight wall down to the yard. Smokey teetered on the edge of the window, his tail flicking anxiously back and forth. He had to get out, and this was the only way. He edged a little further, onto the outside windowsill. He could see all the way down the yard, and he was sure that if he could get down there, he could find his way back to Olivia somehow. But it was a long way to jump.... He paced up and down, meowing pitifully. He was cold out there on the windowsill. The sky was darkening, and there was a chilly wind ruffling his fur. It shook the branches of the tree in the corner of the yard, and they kept tapping against the wall and scraping the windowsill.

Smokey crouched on the windowsill, shivering, and watching the twigs brushing against the wall. It was the only way down, but the branches were like thin little fingers. He had never climbed a tree, and certainly never climbed *down* one.

Suddenly, Smokey whipped around. He could hear the door handle turning. He had to go now! He sprang onto the nearest branch that looked strong enough to hold him and meowed with fright as it wobbled and dipped underneath him. He clung on desperately, digging his claws into the bark, and wailed as a gust of wind shook the tree again.

He scrambled along the branch toward the tree trunk, then skidded and bumped down to the fence, where he perched, meowing with fright. It was a very narrow fence, but at least it wasn't shaking—or at least not as much as the tree had been.

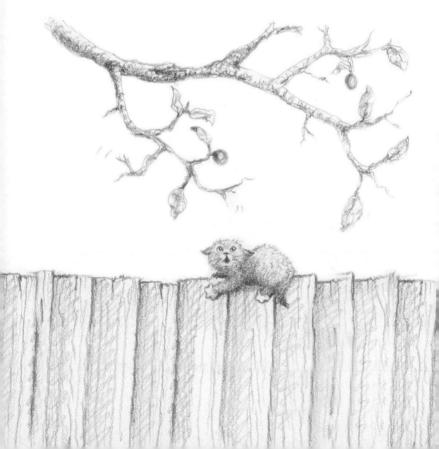

Smokey teetered, trying to figure out which way to jump. Back into the yard? But then the boy might come and find him. Down the other side of the fence? There was long grass down there that looked soft enough to jump onto. But he had no idea where the alley went, or if it would lead to Olivia. There were only a few battered-looking garages.

He jumped, bouncing down the side of the fence, and landing in a flurry of paws on the soft grass. Now where should he go?

"Yes, Rob's here. I'll get him for you, Ben."

Ben put his hand over the phone

89

receiver and nodded to Olivia and Mom. "He's coming."

Olivia sat forward on the couch, trying to listen, and Ben rolled his eyes and pressed the speakerphone button. Rob's voice echoed out into the room.

"What is it?" He sounded jumpy and worried.

"Where's Smokey?" Ben demanded.

"What do you mean?"

"He knows!" Olivia hissed. Rob was trying to sound as though he didn't understand, but he wasn't very good at it.

"We found all your stuff. You took him home in your school bag, didn't you?" Ben said angrily.

"I'm sorry...," Rob muttered finally. "It was all a mistake. Smokey was sniffing around my bag, and then he climbed in and went to sleep. I just wanted to have him for a little bit to see what it would be like...."

"You stole him!" Olivia yelled at the phone. "Bring him back now!"

There was silence. Then Rob whispered, "I can't...."

"What do you mean, you can't?" Ben asked.

"He's gone." Rob sounded almost like he was crying.

"You lost him!" Olivia cried.

"I think he got out my bedroom window," Rob gulped. "He must have. I searched my entire room, and he just wasn't anywhere. I'm sorry."

Mom reached for the phone. "Rob, please get your mother for me."

Olivia didn't even hear as her mom and Rob's mom tried to figure out what was going on. She was slumped on the couch, her hands squashed into her eyes to stop herself from crying.

Eventually Mom ended the call, then put one arm around Olivia and one around Ben.

"It looks like Rob did take Smokey," she said slowly. "His mom said she couldn't believe he'd do something so thoughtless. He hadn't told her what had happened. She's really sorry."

"What are we going to do?" Olivia wailed. "Can we go over to Rob's house and look for Smokey?"

"Rob's dad just came home, and he's going out to look and ask all the neighbors," Mom explained. "I don't think there's much point in us going over there since it's almost dark. Rob's mom said he thinks Smokey must have been gone for about half an hour. He could have gotten away down the street."

"But it's so cold," Olivia whispered. "Smokey is out there all alone!"

Chapter Seven
Trapped!

Smokey was still hiding in the long grass, wondering what to do. He was incredibly hungry. If he was at home, he was sure it would be dinnertime. A bowl of crunchy food, or maybe some of the meaty stuff he really liked. The thought of food made him more determined. He had to go home. He crept out of the clump of grass and looked around the alley worriedly. He had no idea if he was close to Olivia's house or not.

Maybe he could call for Olivia. But then, he was still very close to the house. What if that boy heard him?

He took a few steps down the alley, his fur prickling. The air felt strange, and it was making him edgy. He continued on, hoping desperately that he would see some sign of Olivia. Wouldn't she come and look for him? Now that he was farther away from Rob's house, he risked meowing hopefully. But no one was around to hear him.

A large raindrop landed suddenly on his nose, and he jumped back in surprise. It was followed by another

and another, and in seconds Smokey's
fur was soaked and clinging to him.
The rain was followed by a strange
eerie flash that seemed to split the
dark sky, and then a rolling boom of
thunder. Smokey shot across the alley
to the garages, looking for a place to
hide. They were all locked up, but he
spotted a hole, where a brick had come
loose, and squeezed himself inside.
There was another crash of thunder.
Startled, he jumped back, bumping
into a pile of boxes and paint cans,
which fell clattering all around him.

Smokey scampered away with a
terrified squeak. When he looked back,
he saw that a heavy wooden box had
fallen right in front of his hole. He
was trapped.

He sprang forward, frantically meowing and clawing at the box, but it was much too heavy for him to move.

At last he stopped scratching and sat back, exhausted. He wove his way through the dusty darkness, around the piles of boxes and bikes and all kinds of stuff that was stored in the garage, hoping to find another hole. But he couldn't find even the tiniest gap.

Miserably he settled down on a pile of old drop cloths. It was cold, and he was starving, and he wanted to be on Olivia's lap on the couch. Sadly, he snuffled himself to sleep.

"Look at the rain," Olivia whispered, peering out the living room window.

Mom came up behind her and hugged her. "I'm sure he's tucked himself away somewhere safe. We'll find him tomorrow."

"He's only ever been out in the yard with us." Olivia turned to look at Mom, her eyes wide and worried. "He's never been out in the rain! And the thunder is so scary. He must be terrified."

"Like you," Ben muttered from her doorway. But he didn't seem to be putting much effort into teasing her. He sounded too miserable to bother. He came over to the window and stared at the rain. "Rob's dad called just now. He's asked all the neighbors to keep an eye out for Smokey, but he had to stop looking and come back inside—he said he couldn't see anything because it was raining so hard."

Their dad came in, carrying the phone. "Olivia, it's Hailey on the phone for you."

Olivia took the phone reluctantly. She wasn't sure whether she wanted to talk to Hailey or not. She desperately wanted to tell someone how angry she was with Rob, but at the same time, she didn't want to have to say that Smokey was missing.

"Hi, Olivia! Mom says I can come over to your house tomorrow, if you like. Would that be okay with your mom?"

"I don't know...," Olivia whispered, her eyes prickling with tears.

"Oh, are you going out?" Hailey's voice was disappointed. "I was hoping we could play with Smokey. I really want to see him!"

Olivia sniffed, and then sobbed. "He's gone!"

There was a confused silence on the other end of the line. "You mean, he had to go back to the Rescue Center?" Hailey said at last.

"No. Remember how Rob came over to play with Ben? He took him."

"Rob Ford stole your kitten?" Hailey sounded as though she didn't quite believe it.

Olivia gave an angry little laugh. "I know it sounds silly, but he really did! He even owned up to it. But then Smokey tried to get away from him and climbed out his bedroom window, and now we don't know where he is!"

"What are you going to do?" Hailey whispered in horror.

"We're going to look for him tomorrow—Mom says it's too dark to go over there now. But he could be anywhere, Hailey. And it's a horrible night."

"Can I come and help you look? I bet my mom will come, too. The more people we have looking, the better the chance there is that we'll find him," Hailey suggested.

For the first time since she'd realized Smokey was gone, Olivia felt a little bit better. "Would you really help look?"

"Call me tomorrow and let me know when," Hailey told her firmly. "We'll find him."

"Okay," Olivia whispered. "Thanks, Hailey. See you in the morning." She put the phone down on the table. "Hailey's going to come over tomorrow and help us look," she explained to Mom and Dad.

Dad nodded. "That's nice of her. Look, I think you should go to bed. You're only sitting here making yourself feel worse. And we want to get up early and go and look for Smokey."

Olivia nodded and went up to her room, but she didn't think she'd be able to get to sleep. And when she did, she was sure she was going to dream about Smokey all night. Smokey lost and all alone, and wondering why she hadn't come to find him.

She lay in her warm bed, listening to the rain drumming on the roof outside her window, and hoping that Smokey was hidden somewhere safe. *But he could be anywhere,* she thought worriedly, turning over, and curling up under her comforter. What if they never found him? What would they say to the people from the Rescue Center? Debbie had said they would call in the next few days to see how they were doing, and if Smokey was settling in. They would have to tell her that they had lost him! Or actually, that a selfish boy had stolen him.

Olivia thumped her pillow. At least being angry with Rob had stopped her from wanting to cry. She wondered if someone could be sent to prison for stealing a kitten. Rob certainly deserved it. Dreamily, she imagined Rob in handcuffs, and herself standing there, with Smokey purring in her arms, watching as the police led him away.

It seemed so real. For a moment, she was sure that she could hear Smokey purring. But it was only the rain beating against her window.

Chapter Eight
The Rescue Mission

Smokey woke up shivering. Although he had huddled himself into the pile of drop cloths, it was freezing inside the garage. He felt so cold that he could hardly move. At last he stood up gingerly, stretching out his paws and fluffing up his fur to keep himself as warm as possible. He was sure that he was colder because he was so hungry.

The last food he'd had was the sandwich in that boy's bag yesterday afternoon, and now he felt horribly empty.

It was getting light. There were dirty, grayish windows at the top of the walls, just under the roof, and a little watery sunshine was fighting its way in. Somehow it made Smokey feel more cheerful, even if it wasn't making him much warmer. In the light he could see that the garage was full of piles of old junk—car parts and bikes, piles of paint cans, and lots of dust. Last night, it had just been strange shapes that wobbled when he scurried past them. It was all a lot less scary in the daylight.

He jumped down from his pile of drop cloths, his legs still stiff and achy from the cold, and started to search for a way out. Last night, with the rain pouring down, the garage had at least been a shelter. Now it was stopping him from going home to Olivia, and he was determined to escape. Surely now that it was lighter, he would be able to find another hole somewhere! Smokey made his way along the wall, sniffing and nudging at the concrete blocks.

Edging around the side of a large box, his whiskers twitched hopefully as he spotted a little light coming through a crack at the bottom of the wall. He nosed at it eagerly, and then his whiskers drooped again. It was such a very small gap. But he had to try. The rest of the walls were made from solid concrete blocks, but here one of the blocks seemed to have broken, and it had been patched up with a metal sheet on the outside. If he wriggled into the dark gap between the blocks, there was a tiny hole. Maybe if he clawed at it for a while, it might give way....

Smokey scratched hopefully, his tiny claws making an eerie screeching noise against the rough metal sheet. He scratched and scraped for what seemed like forever, until his claws ached, but when he stopped and pressed his nose against the hole, it didn't seem to have gotten any bigger at all....

"Olivia! What time is it?" Dad moaned.

"Um, five thirty. You said we'd get up early and go straight over to Rob's!"

"I meant more like seven...," Dad muttered wearily.

"Go back to bed until six thirty," Mom added. "We can't go and wake up Rob's family this early."

110

Olivia sighed. She supposed Mom was right. But she had been lying awake since five, watching her bedroom get lighter and lighter. As soon as it seemed to be light enough to search for a kitten, she had gotten up.

She trudged back to her room and lay down on her bed. She wasn't going to be able to go back to sleep. Instead, she grabbed a notebook from her nightstand and started to make a list of things it would be useful to take with them on the search.

A flashlight in case they had to look anywhere dark, Olivia thought. *Behind a shed or something like that. Smokey's favorite snacks.* He really liked the little heart-shaped chicken ones. Olivia had done a taste test on five different kinds, and he always went for the chicken ones first. If he was stuck in a tree or anything like that, he would definitely come down for them.

What else? Olivia chewed the end of her pencil. *A ladder?* She wasn't sure Dad would want to carry one around.

"Oh, you're awake!" Mom put her head around Olivia's door. Olivia gazed up at her. Of course she was! How could she go back to sleep?

"Can I get up now?" she asked eagerly.

Mom nodded. "Yes. But we're not going anywhere until you've had some breakfast. Just a quick bowl of cereal, that's all," she added, seeing Olivia was about to complain. "If you eat, you'll be able to look for him better."

Olivia dressed quickly, and then ran

downstairs to gulp down the bowl of cereal that Mom insisted on. Then she grabbed the flashlight and the snacks and stood by the front door, waiting impatiently for Mom and Dad and Ben.

"What about Hailey?" she asked Mom, who was putting on her coat.

"I texted her mom. It's still only seven-thirty, Olivia, and I didn't want to get her out of bed. But I told her where we'll be; she can call my cell phone if she and Hailey want to come."

Dad gave an enormous yawn. "Everyone ready?"

They met Rob's dad halfway along Rob's street, crouching down to look under a big garbage can.

"No luck yet?" Mom asked.

He shook his head. "Not yet. But he can't have gone far. I'm really sorry about this. Rob feels terrible. He's looking farther up the road with his mom."

He should *feel terrible!* Olivia thought. But being furious with Rob didn't really help.

She and Ben and Mom and Dad set off down the street, calling and peering over fences. Olivia kept shaking the treats, hoping to see a little gray kitten dash eagerly toward her like he did at home.

Half an hour later, they were back outside Rob's house, and everyone looked hopeless. Especially Rob. It seemed like he'd been crying, and Olivia almost felt sorry for him.

"Not a sign," Dad said, frowning. "And none of the people we asked have seen him."

"Should we go farther? The next street?" Rob's mom asked doubtfully.

"Oh, look!" Mom pointed down the street.

"What is it? Can you see him?" Olivia gasped.

"I'm sorry, Olivia. It's only Hailey, down at the end of the street, with her mom."

Hailey came running up the street as soon as she spotted Olivia. "We'll find him," she promised, seeing her friend's disappointed face and hugging her tightly.

"I'm sure we will," her mom agreed

as they reached the little crowd outside Rob's house. "There are a lot of us looking now."

Everyone was still discussing where to look next.

"He couldn't still be in your yard, hidden somewhere?" Olivia suggested.

"We looked. We really did," Rob mumbled.

But his mom nodded. "We did, but if Smokey was frightened, he might have hidden himself. What if Ben and Olivia went and called to him? It's worth a try, anyway." She led them down the side of the house and into the backyard, then went inside to make some tea for everyone.

"Smokey! Smokey!" Olivia shook the cat treats again and again, and

Ben jingled Smokey's favorite ball. Hailey walked around the yard searching under all the bushes. But Smokey didn't appear. The yard was so quiet and empty.

I don't think we're ever going to find him, Olivia thought, staring sadly at the house. She knew Smokey had been here just last night, but he hadn't left even the tiniest clue. "Is that your window?" she asked Rob, who was sitting on the patio. She could see soccer stickers on a window that looked desperately high up. Had Smokey really climbed out of there?

Hailey gulped. "That's so high!"

Rob nodded miserably. "I think he must have jumped into that tree."

The girls went over to look at it. It was a plum tree—they could see the odd

117

fruit still left at the top of the branches. It filled the gap between the house and the fence, and some of the branches spilled over the other side.

"What's over there?" Ben asked, trying to scramble up and grab the top of the fence.

"Just some old garages and stuff. There's an alley that runs from the street behind ours," Rob said. "But the fence is really solid. He couldn't have gotten under it. He must have gone around the side of the house and out the front."

But Olivia stared at the tree and the fence thoughtfully. "What if he didn't go under the fence? Couldn't he have gone over it?"

"Of course not! Look how tall it is…." Ben trailed off. "Oh! From the tree!"

Olivia nodded. "How do we get around there?"

Rob led them around the side of the house, and Ben popped his head through the back door to explain that they were going to look in the alley.

"We'll be just a few minutes," he said quickly, and they vanished into the alley before anyone could stop them.

"Why didn't we think of it before?" Rob muttered as they hurried off. "We just thought he must have gone out the front."

The alley ran along halfway between Rob's house and the one next door, but they had to go into the next street to get into it. It was very narrow, with a row of old garages—and lots of hiding places for a kitten.

"Smokey!" Olivia tore the treats packet open with her teeth and shook out a handful.

Inside the garage, Smokey was pacing up and down by the hole in the wall. He had to keep trying—he had to get out! He scraped determinedly at the metal sheet, ignoring his sore paws. Then his ears pricked up suddenly as he heard the sound of a familiar voice. Was that Olivia? Had she come to find him? He scratched furiously at the wall again, trying to show her where he was.

"Hey, what was that?" Hailey said suddenly. "Something is scratching!"

Everyone froze, holding their breath, waiting for the sound again.

"I can't hear anything!" Ben hissed.

"Shh! Listen! There it is again!" Hailey whispered.

Olivia jumped, dropping half the treats on the ground. "I heard it, too! It must be him. Smokey, where are you?" she called.

There was silence for a minute, and then a loud, desperate meow.

"It is! It is! Where is he? Smokey,

we're coming to find you!" Olivia called, running toward the garages.

Inside the garage, Smokey scratched at the metal again. He could hear Olivia! She'd was going to rescue him. Furiously he scraped and scratched, meowing as loudly as he could. He had to make her hear him!

"Which one is it?" Ben asked.

"The one at the end, I think," Rob said, smiling for the first time that morning. "He must be stuck somehow, and he's trying to get out."

Olivia pushed her way past him and crouched down by the garage wall. "He's here somewhere. Smokey... Smokey...."

A little gray paw suddenly stuck out from a hole in the concrete wall, where it had been patched together.

"He's there! I saw him. Oh, Smokey, we've missed you!" Olivia petted the grubby little paw. "Look, his claws are all torn where he's been trying to get out." She sniffed, choking back sudden tears.

"How are we going to get him out?" Ben asked. "That hole isn't big enough."

"What about this?" Rob held up a thick stick, which he'd found lying on the grass. "Couldn't we use it to pull that metal away a little more?" He banged gently on the metal sheet, and the paw shot back inside as Smokey jumped back in fright.

"Don't scare him!" Olivia snapped.

Rob shook his head. "I had to, Olivia. If he was right behind the metal, I might hurt his paws with the stick."

"Oh." Olivia nodded.

Rob hooked the stick into the hole and pulled. There was a creaking noise, and the thin metal bent a little.

"It's getting bigger! Here, I'll pull too." Ben added his weight to the stick, and Olivia knelt down by the hole.

"Don't be scared, Smokey! You'll be out of there in a minute."

"There!" Ben said triumphantly. "That must be big enough. Good plan, Rob!"

Inside the garage, Smokey blinked at the hole, his whiskers quivering excitedly. He could hear Olivia. He edged forward, squeezing himself tightly against the concrete block, and suddenly tumbled forward out of the hole and into Olivia's hands.

"Oh, Smokey, we've been looking everywhere." Olivia snuggled the kitten up against her chin, laughing and crying at the same time.

"Hey! You found him!" Olivia's dad came running up the alley, with all the others hurrying behind him.

"He's fine," Olivia told them. "Just a little dirty. He was stuck in that garage."

"We moved that metal sheet. It was Rob who thought of it," Ben explained.

"But he wouldn't have run off and

gotten stuck if I hadn't taken him first," Rob muttered. "I'll never do anything that awful again, I promise."

"You're just lucky that you found him," his dad pointed out grimly.

"I know it was all my fault," Rob muttered. "I said I'm really sorry, Dad."

"I think you'd better give some of your allowance to the Rescue Center as an apology," his mom suggested, and Rob nodded.

Olivia looked at Rob. "He only did it because he really wants a cat of his own," she said.

Rob's dad sighed. "Well, maybe when he proves he can be responsible enough to take care of a kitten, he can have one. Which will take a long time!"

Olivia turned to Rob. "Rob, do you

want to pet Smokey, too?"

Rob ran a gentle finger down the back of Smokey's head.

"Thanks," he whispered.

Now that she had Smokey snuggled up and purring in her arms again, Olivia felt like she could forgive anything. Smokey pressed closer against her, looking nervously at Rob.

"It's okay, Smokey." She tickled him under the chin. "Rob's not going to hurt you." She smiled at Rob, only a small smile, but she got a huge one back.

Hailey reached out to rub Smokey's ears. "He's handsome. You're so lucky, Olivia!"

Olivia smiled. She was. Lucky to have Smokey—and even more lucky to have him back safe.